HAPPY BIRTHDAY KYEISHA

A Birthday
Story

Written by:
Lana Jean Mitchell
Illustrated By: JoelRay Pellerin

Print information available on the last page

Rev. date: 03/10/2016

To order additional copies of this book, contact:
Xlibris
1-888-795-4274
www.Xlibris.com
Orders@Xlibris.com

DEDICATION

This book is dedicated to everyone with a Happy Birthday story.

ACKNOWLEDGEMENT

Thank you to everyone who has encouraged me in my writing and who has helped in the publishing of this book; my family, my mentors, teachers, publishers and well-wishers.

HAPPY BIRTHDAY KYEISHA

A Birthday
Story

Written by:
Lana Jean Mitchell
Illustrated By: JoelRay Pellerin

"**G**irl! I don't think that calendar is going to last until your birthday. The way you keep looking at it, you're going to look all of the dates right off the paper! Ha-ha-ha." "He-he-he." That was my grandmother, Mrs. Gail Goody talking. We call her Grandma Gail. The other person laughing is my mother, Grandma Gail and Granddad Goody's baby girl, Shauna.

Grandma Gail and Granddad Goody have seven children: three girls and four boys. My mother brought me, my brother Patrice, and little sister Dara to visit Grandma Gail today.

Granddad Goody says, "He has almost enough children for a baseball team, like his favorite team, the Detroit Stars. They played in the Negro League in 1961." My mother and grandma Gail are talking about my birthday cupcakes.

In three days I will be eight, and I'm having a birthday party at Rosa Parks Elementary school in Ms. Pushem's third-grade class. I can hardly wait! When someone has a birthday in our class, they can have a party, if their parents bring everything.

So Grandma Gail is baking my cupcakes. She says I can have any kind I want. I'm having two kind: one and a half dozen double Dutch chocolate with fudge icing and one and a half dozen lemon with honey glaze frosting. "Um-m-m-m." I'll have enough for everyone to have one of each, if they want.

I asked Grandma Gail to put rainbow sprinkles on top of all of my cupcakes. These are Grandma Gail's best cupcakes. She makes them from "scratch." She uses her hand mixer to beat together the butter, sugar, flour, eggs, and other stuff. If I'm around when she's finished, I get to lick the spoon and the bowl.

But I won't be around to get the spoon and bowl for my birthday cupcakes, because I have only 2 days left before my birthday. So, tomorrow after school, mama and I will go to the grocery store to buy the ice cream, and soda for the punch. I told my best friend Tamara at recess today, that we will buy one individual cup of vanilla ice cream for each person in my class. The punch will have lemon soda and ice cream too.

I told my best friend Tamara at recess today that we will buy one individual cup of vanilla ice cream for each person in my class. The punch will have lemon soda and ice cream too. Mama said I need to have plates, spoons, cups, and napkins to serve the cupcakes, ice cream, and punch. We will go to the Party Place and get the ones with the picture of Harriet Tubman.

Harriet Tubman was a famous African American. I am African American too. Harriet Tubman was born enslaved a long time ago. She ran away to freedom, and she helped other enslaved people become free.

I got her doll for a Kwanzaa gift from my dad. His name is James Jr. The Party Place has balloons. My mother ordered yellow, green, and red balloons with "HAPPY BIRTHDAY, KYEISHA" on them.

Martin, my big brother, is bringing his video camera to the party to make a video for me to keep forever!

On Thursday, the day before my birthday party, Mama is taking me to the mall to buy a birthday outfit. I'll wear it for the party.

I want a pair of yellow shorts with a matching top. Tamara said yellow looks good with my tan sandals. Yellow is my favorite color.

Mama said if I have birthday cupcakes and ice cream left from my party, I can share it with Patrice and Dara and the rest of the family.

Do you see why I can hardly wait? Do you see why I keep looking at the calendar? Wouldn't it be hard for you to wait?

Printed in the United States
By Bookmasters